RIVERDALE

STUDENT HANDBOOK

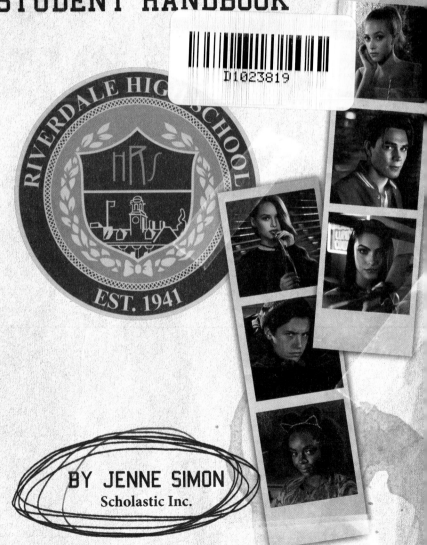

RIVERDALE HIGH SCHOOL

HRS

EST. 1941

D1023819

BY JENNE SIMON

Scholastic Inc.

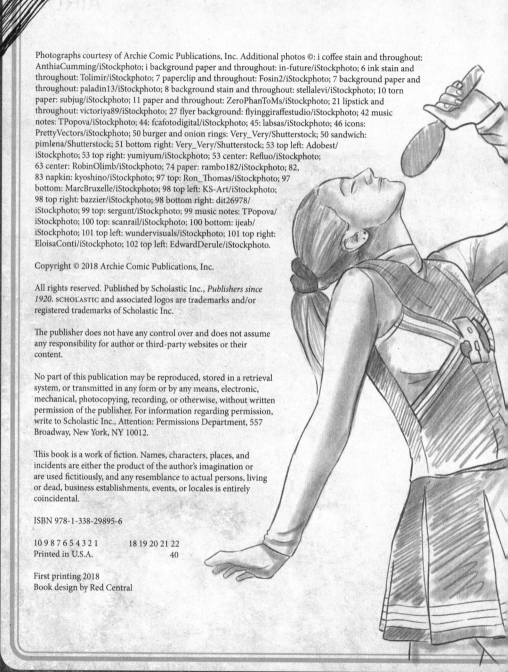

Photographs courtesy of Archie Comic Publications, Inc. Additional photos ©: i coffee stain and throughout:
AnthiaCumming/iStockphoto; i background paper and throughout: in-future/iStockphoto; 6 ink stain and
throughout: Tolimir/iStockphoto; 7 paperclip and throughout: Fosin2/iStockphoto; 7 background paper and
throughout: paladin13/iStockphoto; 8 background stain and throughout: stellalevi/iStockphoto; 10 torn
paper: subjug/iStockphoto; 11 paper and throughout: ZeroPhanToMs/iStockphoto; 21 lipstick and
throughout: victoriya89/iStockphoto; 27 flyer background: flyinggiraffestudio/iStockphoto; 42 music
notes: TPopova/iStockphoto; 44: fcafotodigital/iStockphoto; 45: labsas/iStockphoto; 46 icons:
PrettyVectors/iStockphoto; 50 burger and onion rings: Very_Very/Shutterstock; 50 sandwich:
pimlena/Shutterstock; 51 bottom right: Very_Very/Shutterstock; 53 top left: Adobest/
iStockphoto; 53 top right: yumiyum/iStockphoto; 53 center: Refluo/iStockphoto;
63 center: RobinOlimb/iStockphoto; 74 paper: rambo182/iStockphoto; 82,
83 napkin: kyoshino/iStockphoto; 97 top: Ron_Thomas/iStockphoto; 97
bottom: MarcBruxelle/iStockphoto; 98 top left: KS-Art/iStockphoto;
98 top right: bazzier/iStockphoto; 98 bottom right: dit26978/
iStockphoto; 99 top: sergunt/iStockphoto; 99 music notes: TPopova/
iStockphoto; 100 top: scanrail/iStockphoto; 100 bottom: ijeab/
iStockphoto; 101 top left: wundervisuals/iStockphoto; 101 top right:
EloisaConti/iStockphoto; 102 top left: EdwardDerule/iStockphoto.

ISBN 978-1-338-29895-6

10 9 8 7 6 5 4 3 2 1   18 19 20 21 22
Printed in U.S.A.   40

First printing 2018
Book design by Red Central

CONTENTS

don't know if you've heard, but lately things have been getting weird around here.

CONTENTS CONTINUED

BLEH

Go Bulldogs!

You haven't seen anything yet.

RIVERDALE
HIGH SCHOOL

Dear ~~Students~~, SHEEP

Welcome to Riverdale High School! Our mission is to foster curiosity, strength of character, and connection to the community. We aim to help you grow into lifelong learners and critical thinkers through rigorous interdisciplinary study in the arts, sciences, humanities, and physical education.

MAYBE A LITTLE TOO EAGER

Our faculty is eager to help you reach your full potential. At Riverdale, we have high expectations of our students because we believe that you can do anything you set your mind to if you feel empowered and supported.

So strap on your thinking caps, take out your books, and get ready for a ~~wonderful~~ school year!

INSANE

Sincerely

Waldo Weatherbee

Waldo Weatherbee
~~Principal~~ WARDEN

WHO IS THE
SUGARMAN?

1

This place is like the lost epilogue of _Our Town_.

OUR HISTORY

Riverdale High School was founded in 1941, with local businessman Calvin Merriweather serving as principal. What originated as the only public secondary school in Rockland County is now a vibrant campus of approximately 1,100 students.

In 1953, Don Moore took the reins and set forth a new school's motto: Fostering excellence through knowledge, character, and integrity. This is the guiding legacy that shapes the school's culture of champions, and one the school's eighth principal, Waldo Weatherbee, continues to uphold to this day.

Situated on Pine Avenue in downtown Riverdale, our beautiful campus features state-of-the art classrooms, well-kept athletic fields, and a wealth of historic moments that will live on in Riverdale for years to come.

CAMPUS MAP

The best
Southside spot!

IN THE NEWS RHS GOSSIP

As told to Veronica Lodge

At Riverdale High School, we believe in shining a light on the accomplishments of our students. Here are a few recent and noteworthy moments we'd like to spotlight:

~~The Riverdale Bulldogs have beaten our archrivals from Southside High on the football field for the last ten years.~~

Reggie Mantle was only chosen football captain because dear, sweet Archiekins passed it up.

~~The orchestra will be playing an upcoming concert in Greendale to benefit the Sweetwater River Cleanup Commission.~~

Ms. Grundy resigned because she was giving very private lessons.

~~Coach Clayton was named football coach of the year by the Rockland County Athletic Association.~~

Junior Chuck Clayton was named douche of the year by yours truly. Good thing it only takes a hot tub and a cell phone video to keep him in line.

THE BLUE & GOLD

THE WEEKLY NEWSPAPER OF RIVERDALE HIGH SCHOOL

RIVERDALE STUDENT FOUND FLOATING IN SWEETWATER RIVER

By Betty Cooper

Jason Blossom's body was found floating in the Sweetwater River on July 11th. He was previously believed to have drowned while boating with twin sister Cheryl Blossom. But sources say Jason's death was no accident. One of the unnamed students who discovered the body claims he saw a bullet hole between Jason's eyes. We can only assume that it was not self-inflicted.

ADMINISTRATION

The main office is open from 7:30 a.m. to 4:30 p.m. Monday through Friday. Students needing to purchase parking passes, turn in doctor's notes, or make an appointment with the guidance counselor, Mrs. Burble, should do so during these times. All guests must check in at the office when first entering the campus. No unauthorized persons are allowed on the property at any time!

Not that that's ever stopped my mother, Madame Mayor.

ARE YOU READY TO RIDE OR DIE?

SOUTHSIDE

SERPENTS

SERPENT LAWS

1. A SERPENT NEVER SHOWS COWARDICE.

2. IF A SERPENT'S KILLED OR IMPRISONED, THEIR FAMILY WILL BE TAKEN CARE OF.

3. NO SERPENT STANDS ALONE.

SERPENT LAWS

4. NO SERPENT IS LEFT FOR DEAD.

5. A SERPENT NEVER BETRAYS THEIR OWN.

6. IN UNITY, THERE IS STRENGTH.

THE SOUTHSIDE SERPENTS ARE MORE THAN A CLUB. WE'RE A FAMILY. AND WE PROTECT OUR OWN. THINK YOU HAVE WHAT IT TAKES TO JOIN US? YOU'LL HAVE TO GUARD THE BEAST, GRAB THE KNIFE, HANDLE A SNAKE-BITE, AND SURVIVE THE GAUNTLET.

IF YOU THINK YOU'RE TOUGH ENOUGH, COME BY THE WHYTE WYRM AND ASK FOR TALL BOY.

CODE OF CONDUCT

We expect our students to conduct themselves with dignity, respect the rules of the institution, and adhere to a strict academic honesty policy that precludes cheating and plagiarism. Violators will be disciplined.

Weekdays from 8:25 a.m. to 3:00 p.m. we adhere to a strict regimen. Everything in our lives is controlled. But then something like the murder of Jason Blossom happens, and you realize there is no such thing as control. There is only chaos. Nevertheless, some of us strive to impose and maintain order in what is, fundamentally, an orderless world.
—Jughead Jones

SCHOOL STORE

The school store is located in the administrative offices, and is open during school hours to sell Riverdale High merchandise, as well as tickets for shows, concerts, and other school events.

You'll look like a sheep . . . But a popular sheep at least.

Perfect for covering up yesterday's outfit on the walk of shame.

I'd never wear anything without a designer label. But if you dress like a hobo (read: Jughead) or a bride of hobo (aka Betty), you might want to cover up your peasant garb.

11

SCHOOL SPIRIT

Our hearts ring true to the gold and blue! Support your Riverdale Bulldogs at pep rallies. Cheer them on at games against our archrivals, the Baxter High Ravens of Greendale. And show your school spirit by singing the Riverdale fight song loud and proud.

"OUR FAIR RIVERDALE"

ALL HAIL
OUR FAIR RIVERDALE.
MY HEART RINGS TRUE
TO THE GOLD AND BLUE
WHERE FRIENDSHIPS STARTED,
<u>NEAR OR PARTED,</u>
<u>ALWAYS STAY WITH YOU.</u>

WHEN DAYS TURN TO MEMORY,
THE PAST OF DAWN—
WHAT WAS, WAS NOW GONE.
THE STORMS WE WEATHER,
STRONG TOGETHER,
BOUND TO CARRY ON.

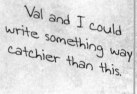

Val and I could write something way catchier than this.

ALL HAIL
OUR FAIR RIVERDALE.
MY HEART RINGS TRUE
TO THE GOLD AND BLUE
WHERE FRIENDSHIPS STARTED,
NEAR OR PARTED,
ALWAYS STAY WITH YOU.

MEET THE FACULTY

The educators and staff at Riverdale High School are thrilled to help you pursue academic and social excellence.

WALDO WEATHERBEE
PRINCIPAL

COACH CLAYTON
TEACHER / FOOTBALL COACH

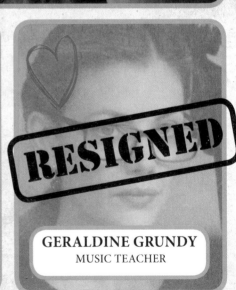

RESIGNED

GERALDINE GRUNDY
MUSIC TEACHER

MISSING IMAGE DUE TO
ABSENCE ON PICTURE DAY.

Ms. BELL
RECEPTIONIST

ALICE COOPER
NEWSPAPER ADVISOR

JOSEPH SVENSON
JANITOR

MISSING IMAGE DUE TO
ABSENCE ON PICTURE DAY.

Mrs. BURBLE
GUIDANCE COUNSELOR

MEET FELLOW STUDENTS

As you acclimate to life at RHS, look to our current students for models of exemplary Bulldog behavior.

Name:	**ARCHIBALD ANDREWS**
Favorite Subject:	Music
Activities:	Bulldog football, songwriting
Hero:	John Lennon
Quote:	"You can't go through life trying not to get hurt."

Archie

Nickname: Justin Gingerlake

Name:	**CHERYL BLOSSOM**
Favorite Subject:	History
Activities:	River Vixens, Student Government
Hero:	Eva Perón
Quote:	"If you breathe, it's because I give you air."

HBIC

As hot and smart as Betty is, she should be the Queen Bey of this drab hive.

Crazier than a seria killer on bath salts.

Name:	~~ELIZABETH~~ BETTY COOPER DARK BETTY LIVES!!
Favorite Subject:	All of them
Activities:	*Blue & Gold* editor-in-chief, Honor Association, River Vixens
Hero:	Toni Morrison
Quote:	"I learned that from the Nancy Drew detective handbook."

Name: ~~FORSYTHE~~ ~~PENDLETON~~ JONES III
JUGHEAD

Favorite Subject: English

Activities: none

Hero: Jack Kerouac

Quote: "I'm not wired to be normal."

JUGHEAD =
SERPENT

Name:	**KEVIN KELLER**
Favorite Subject:	Math
Activities:	wrestling team, AV Club
Hero:	Neil Patrick Harris
Quote:	"Is cheerleading even still a thing?"

tl;dr: Boring.

Name:	**VERONICA LODGE**
Favorite Subject:	Spanish
Activities:	River Vixens, Community Service Club
Hero:	Coco Chanel
Quote:	"I don't follow rules, I make them. When necessary, I break them."

NEW GIRL

MEET FELLOW STUDENTS

JOSIE
AND THE
PUSSYCATS

Named for
Josephine Baker,
another seriously
talented songstres

Name:	**JOSIE McCOY**
Favorite Subject:	Music
Activities:	Josie and the Pussycats
Hero:	Diana Ross
Quote:	"Don't stare at our Pussycat ears. It's rude."

My girl! ♡

JASON BLOSSOM

VALERIE BROWN

MEET FELLOW STUDENTS

I hear Dilton knows his way around the Sweetwater River.

His conversation's not exactly the stuff of Oscar Wilde. Or even Diablo Cody.

DILTON DOILEY

MIDGE KLUMP

CHUCK CLAYTON

REGGIE MANTLE

I hear Reggie knows his way around jingle-jangle...

Moose is hot, but he's got more demons than <u>The Exorcist</u>.

MOOSE MASON

ETHEL MUGGS

MELODY VALENTINE

Fangs Fogarty

STUDENT RECORDS

Student records are stored in the principal's office. Students have the right to inspect records, challenge content, and control the disclosure of information.

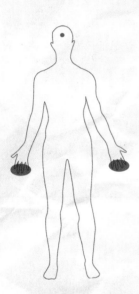

<u>Office of the Riverdale Medical Examiner</u>
Case No. 935-592
Report of Investigation

Decedent: Jason Blossom   **Sex:** Male   **Age:** 16
Home Address: Thornhill Manor   **Occupation:** Student

Type of Death:
- ☐ Violent
- ☐ Casualty
- ☐ Suicide
- ☐ Suddenly when in apparent health
- ☐ Found dead
- ☐ In prison
- ☑ Suspicious, unusual, or unnatural

Investigating Agency: Sheriff's office

Description of Body:
- ☑ Clothed
- ☐ Unclothed
- ☐ Partially Clothed

Eyes: Blue   **Mustache:** No   **Beard:** No
Hair: Red   **Height:** 6'1"   **Weight:** 185

Marks and Wounds: Bullet hole in forehead, frostbite on hands, waterlogged skin

Probable Cause of Death: Homicide

GRAD REQUIREMENTS

Riverdale High students are expected to obtain a minimum of 32 credits and maintain a 2.7 average to earn their diploma.

LET'S
SHOWER

Polly Cooper

WITH GIFTS &
HELP HER CELEBRATE
HER LITTLE MIRACLES

SUNDAY OCTOBER 22
2 O'CLOCK
THE PEMBROOKE

HOSTED BY
BETTY COPPER &
HERMIONE LODGE

SAFETY

Riverdale High conducts drills throughout the year so students and faculty alike can be prepared in the event of an emergency. As some of you may know, Riverdale has had a higher crime rate as of late. Your safety is our biggest priority.

And I thought New York City was dangerous...

RIVERDALE is NOT inNOcenT.
iT's A ToWN oF hYPOCRiTEs,
dEGenERaTEs, aND CriMiNaLs.
MY WRath is THE PRiCE
oF yoUR LiEs. yoUR SECRETs.
yoUR sins.

i WiLL NOT STOP.
i CANNOT BE SToPPEd.
i AM THE WoLF.
YOU aRE THE FLOCK.
This is THE bLOODLETTinG.

yoU WiLL
hEAR FRoM ME aGain.

DRESS CODE

In order to maintain a positive educational environment, students must adhere to the following standards of attire, and may not wear anything revealing, lewd, or offensive at any time.

- No hats, hoods, bandanas, or sunglasses.
- Shirts must be worn and buttoned at all times. *This goes without saying*
- No visible bra straps.
- Pants must be worn at the waist or above.
- No perfume or cologne.
- Skirts should be no shorter than two inches above the knee. *What is this, 1956?*
- Sneakers must be clean.
- All other shoes should have a heel of 1" or lower.

Only if you're going to the beach.

LODGE
INDUSTRIES

Veronica's Rules for Making a Fashionable First Impression

Pearls are a timeless classic.

Shop Givenchy and Oscar de la Renta when you're flush.

Keep it clean and ladylike even when you're not.

Your signature color should make you feel powerful.

If you've got it, flaunt it.

The higher the heel, the closer to heaven.

You can never go wrong with a spritz of Chanel No. 5.

Quality. Always.

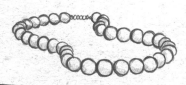

LOCKERS

Every student will be assigned a locker for his or her personal use throughout the school year. Riverdale High School assumes no responsibility for lost or stolen articles taken from lockers. DO NOT leave valuables such as money, electronic devices, jewelry, or anything of particular sentimental value in your locker at any time.

THE GREAT
OUTDOORS

SOUTHSIDE
SERPEN

CHANEL

ATTENDANCE

Daily attendance is essential for learning. All students are expected to attend classes regularly and in a timely manner.

ATTENDANCE

Name	Week 1					Week 2					Week 3				
	M	T	W	T	F	M	T	W	T	F	M	T	W	T	F
Andrews, Archie	X	X	X	A	X	X	X	X	X	X	X	X	X	X	X
Blossom, Cheryl	X	X	X	X	X	X	X	A	X	X	X	X	X	X	X
Blossom, Jason	A	A	A	A	A	A	A	A	A	A	A	A	A	A	A
Brown, Trev	X	X	X	X	X	X	X	X	X	X	X	X	X	X	X
Brown, Valerie	X	X	X	X	X	X	X	X	X	X	X	X	X	X	X
Clayton, Chuck	X	X	X	X	X	X	X	X	X	X	X	X	X	X	X
Cooper, Betty	X	X	X	X	X	X	X	X	X	X	X	X	X	X	X
Doiley, Dilton	X	X	X	X	X	X	X	X	X	X	X	X	X	X	X
Jones, Jughead	X	X	X	X	X	X	X	X	X	X	X	A	A	A	X
Keller, Kevin	X	X	X	X	X	X	X	X	X	X	X	X	X	X	X
Klump, Midge	X	X	X	X	X	X	X	X	X	X	X	X	X	X	X
Lodge, Veronica	X	X	X	X	X	X	X	X	X	X	X	X	X	X	X
Lopez, Ginger	X	X	X	X	X	X	X	X	X	X	X	X	X	X	A
Mantle, Reggie	X	X	X	X	X	X	X	X	X	X	X	X	X	X	X
Mason, Moose	X	X	X	X	X	X	X	X	X	X	X	X	X	X	X
McCoy, Josie	X	X	X	X	X	X	X	X	X	A	X	X	X	X	X
Muggs, Ethel	X	X	X	X	X	X	X	X	X	X	X	X	X	X	X
Patel, Tina	X	X	X	X	X	X	X	X	X	X	X	X	X	X	X
Valentine, Melody	X	X	X	X	X	X	X	X	X	X	X	X	X	X	X

My dear sweet Jay-Jay is never coming back

I had a meeting with a producer from Shabbey Road Studios. Don't tell the Pussycats!

HALL PASSES

Unless they are facing a medical emergency, students must obtain a pass to leave class for any reason. Passes are issued at the sole discretion of Riverdale's faculty, and may be revoked at any time.

RIVERDALE
HIGH SCHOOL
OFFICIAL TRANSFER FORM

Name: Forsythe Pendleton Jones III (aka Jughead)

Current School: Riverdale High School

Transferring To: Southside High School

Reason for Transfer: Father was arrested. Mother lives out of state. Will be placed in foster care with a family on the Southside

Concerns: Family has ties to the Southside Serpents. Monitor for gang involvement.

Status: Approved

BULLYING

Good thing she didn't find out about the rumble between us and the Serpents...

Riverdale High takes a zero tolerance approach to bullying. Harassment, intimidation, or physical conflict between students is strictly prohibited.

THE RIVERDALE REGISTER

NORTHSIDE TEEN STABBED BY SOUTHSIDE SERPENT

by Alice Cooper

Last night, Riverdale High student Dilton Doiley was stabbed by the Southside Serpents. This most recent incident confirms that the real threat is not the Black Hood, but the Southside and its corruptive forces. Developer and ex-con Hiram Lodge boasts that his SoDale project will revitalize the forsaken neighborhood, but this reporter speculates Hiram Lodge doesn't want to fix our problems, merely profit from them.

LOST AND FOUND

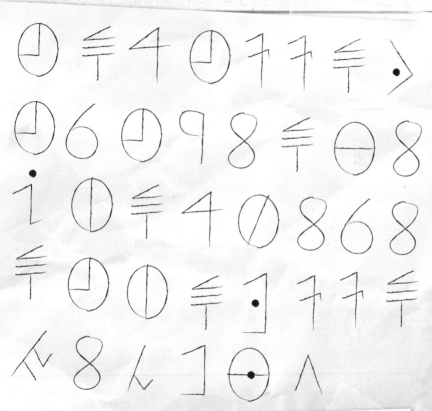

TESTING

Riddle me this—is my mother donatin[g] another wing to the school in Jason's honor or is she just spying on me?

Students will be evaluated with quizzes, essays, and tests, at our faculty's discretion. All courses will culminate with final assessment at the end of the semester. Students who do not receive passing marks must repeat the class in summer school.

Principal Weatherbee's schedule
Wednesday, October 11

9:00 a.m.	Monthly meeting with Superintendent
10:00 a.m.	Parent conference with Alice Cooper
11:00 a.m.	Review Blossom case with Sheriff Keller
12:00 p.m.	Paperwork
1:00 p.m.	Lunch with Penelope Blossom
2:00 p.m.	Consult with security firm on campus safety
3:00 p.m.	See Coach Clayton about Bulldog prospects
4:00 p.m.	Give interview to the *Blue & Gold*
5:00 p.m.	Mayor McCoy wants a private word

COURSE OFFERINGS

7 subjects x 3 semesters = too boring to bother

We believe in a classical, well-rounded education that opens minds, challenges assumptions, and gives our students the foundation they need to go anywhere they choose to in life. Students are required to take at least three classes in each of the following subject areas: English, history, science, math, foreign languages, arts, and physical education.

¿Donde esta el baño?

Except when the assumptions we challenge are theirs.

ENGLISH

English classes include the study of American, English, and world literatures, as well as the development of expository, argumentative, and creative writing skills.

Untitled Poem
by Ethel Muggs

They put me in a wooden box

As I desperately opposed,

But all my screaming was for naught.

My mouth had been sewn closed.

Curled up in bed was just a girl,

Needing Daddy's arms to hold her.

PHYSICAL EDUCATION

Students may elect to take general physical education classes that will engage them in sports and activities to promote a healthy and active lifestyle. Or they may choose to join one of our many teams (football, basketball, baseball/softball, tennis, cross-country/track, volleyball, soccer, or swimming) to earn their PE credits.

MUSIC PROGRAM

Our award-winning music program offers courses in music appreciation, composition, music technology, and technique. Students will study the masters from Beethoven to the Beatles, practice their chosen instruments, and compose original scores.

THE BRANDENBURG MUSIC ACADEMY
SUMMER PROGRAM APPLICATION

NAME: Archie Andrews

AGE: 16

FROM: Riverdale

INSTRUMENTS: guitar (acoustic and electric)

MUSICAL GENRES: rock and pop mostly

AWARDS: None but I've played live with Josie and the Pussycats

SPECIAL SKILLS:

My songwriting is coming along, production skills are decent, and I've been told I have a nice singing voice.

WHY ARE YOU INTERESTED IN OUR SUMMER PROGRAM?

I love music more than anything and I want to devote my life to it. But my music teacher just left town, and I could really use some guidance from professionals.

RECOMMENDED BY: Penelope Blossom

STATUS: Recommendation rescinded—the candidate is not exceptional

APPLICATION STATUS:
- ☐ ACCEPTED
- ☐ WAIT-LISTED
- ☒ DENIED

Whoopsie! I guess that's what happens when you defy Mother Blossom and refuse to date me.

HOME ECONOMICS

It may seem retro, but a good foundation in home economics can serve our students well throughout their lives. This program focuses on five areas of study: finance, textiles, wellness, cooking, and nutrition. *EW*

Featuring a performance by

JOSIE AND THE PUSSYCATS

taste of
Riverdale

Presented by Mayor
Sierra McCoy
in celebration of Riverdale's 75th Anniversary Jubilee.

A four-star **FEAST**ival of food, friendship, and fun!

Pop's Chock'lit Shoppe
Maison Pierre
Lulu Tortilla
The Lobster Shack

Mama Carmela's
Medium Rare
Southern Hospitality
Sushi Tango

MATHEMATICS

All students are required to pass classes in algebra, geometry, and pre-calculus. Our mathematics program is designed to teach theory as well as practical applications to bring the relevance of concepts into students' everyday lives.

RIVERDALE
SHERIFF'S DEPARTMENT
OFFICIAL CRIMINAL RECORD

Name: Hiram Lodge
Case No.: 931-824B
Gender: Male
Age: 46
Known Residence:
The Pembrooke, Riverdale;
formerly of New York City
Status:
Time has been served, on probation.

Offenses:

embezzlement
tax evasion
bribery
extortion

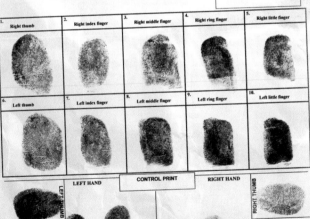

1. Right thumb	2. Right index finger	3. Right middle finger	4. Right ring finger	5. Right little finger
6. Left thumb	7. Left index finger	8. Left middle finger	9. Left ring finger	10. Left little finger

LEFT HAND   CONTROL PRINT   RIGHT HAND

LEFT THUMB   RIGHT THUMB

NEWSPAPER

Our journalism program has recently been reinstated with Betty Cooper leading the charge as the editor-in-chief of Riverdale High's weekly newspaper, the *Blue & Gold*. Advising the newspaper staff is Betty's mother, Alice Cooper, whose experience writing for the *Riverdale Register* is sure to prove essential. Students will learn the basics of investigative journalism including researching articles, interviewing witnesses, and crafting a story.

SCORPIO
(October 23 – November 21)
You will struggle to make a wise decision about your future. However, gathering information will only add to your uncertainty. Trust your intuition.

SAGITTARIUS
(November 22 – December 21)
Don't use humor or philosophy to avoid your feelings after an intense situation arises. If you reveal your true emotions, you will encourage others to do the same.

CAPRICORN
(December 22 – January 19)
Unresolved relationship issues are in the spotlight today. Someone close to you will expose buried feelings. Don't push them away. Let love overpower fear.

AQUARIUS
(January 20 – February 18)
Your open mind makes you incredibly receptive to suggestions. But be sure to check in with yourself or you could be led off the path you are walking.

All right, Betty. You win. No more wandering Fox Forest late at night, no matter how cute the company.

THE BLUE & GOLD

THE WEEKLY NEWSPAPER OF RIVERDALE HIGH SCHOOL

ALICE COOPER'S SECRET SERPENT PAST

by Betty Cooper

Alice Cooper, local reporter for the *Riverdale Register* and advisor to this paper, has been keeping a secret. In her youth, Cooper was a member of the Southside Serpents, a gang he now frequently targets in editorials. Does Cooper have unfinished business with the erpents? Could the reason she blames them r so many of Riverdale's problems be rooted a personal vendetta? Only one thing is rtain: Snakes don't shed their skin easily.

— But sardonic humor is my way of relating to the world!

TUTORING

Students requiring a bit of extra help in their studies have lots of options to get back on track. Ms. Paroo at the library offers regular tutoring appointments after school. Members of the Riverdale Honor Association offer peer-tutoring sessions in every subject.

Teachers may also schedule independent studies ~
discretion to help students who may b
who
area:

Teacher: Geraldine Grundy **Course:** Independent Stu

Student	Semester	Hours per week	Essay #1	Mid Term
Yoshido, Tomoko	Spring	2	C+	B-
Blossom, Jason	Spring	2		A
Andrews, Archie	Fall	5		B+

nal	Special Project	Notes	Grade
B	Cello Sonata	Tomoko's composition is lovely and restrained, but he needs to practice technique—his fingering skills and bow handling need work.	C+
B	Piano concerto	Jason has a good ear, but he doesn't practice enough. He seems distracted . . .	B
B+	A	Guitar composition	Archie has...strong hands and good instincts.	A+

CAFETERIA

All students should be able to enjoy a clean, healthy environm~~~
relax, eat, and socialize. Hot lunc~~~ ~~~
are provided f~~~

POP'S CHOCK 'LIT SHOPPE

**OPEN 24 HRS
7 DAYS A WEEK**

So much better than school lunch

SA~~~

All Sandwiches Served with Coleslaw,
Choice of Bread: Wheat, White, Multi-~~~

Chicken Club
Grilled Chicken, American Cheese, Le~~~

Turkey Club
Turkey, American Cheese, Lettuce, T~~~

Reuben
Roast Beef, Grilled Onions, Russian~~~

Turkey Bacon Avocado
Turkey, American Cheese, Lettuce~~~

Grilled Vegetable
Eggplant, Zucchini, Mushroom, R~~~

Grilled Cheese...........................

BURGERS

All Burgers Come with Coleslaw, Pickle and French Fries.
Substitute Sweet Potato, Waffle, or Curly Fries....$1.00

Pop's Classic $6.00
100% Beef Patty, Lettuce, Tomato, Pickle

Pop's Classic with Cheese $7.00
100% Beef Patty, American Cheese, Lettuce, Tomato, Pickle

Bacon Cheeseburger $10.00
100% Beef Patty, Bacon, American Cheese, Lettuce, Tomato, Pickle

Sweet Water Barbecue Burger $15.00
100% Beef Patty, Lettuce, Tomato, Fried Onions, and Sweetwater
Maple-infused Barbecue Sauce

WHAT HAPPENED TO MR. BLOSSOM?

SIDES

French Fries $2.00
Sweet Potato Fries $3.00
Curly Fries $3.00
Waffle Fries $3.00
Onion Rings $4.00
Coleslaw $2.00

SALADS

Add Chicken, Turkey, Beef, or~~~
Dressings: Ranch, Honey Mu~~~
Bleu Cheese, Carrot Ginger

House Salad
Mixed Greens, Carrots, Tom~~~

Caesar Salad
Lettuce, Parmesan Cheese~~~

Greek Salad
Mixed Greens, Cucumber~~~

Cobb Salad
Lettuce, Baby Spinach, ~~~
Hard-Boiled Egg, Crouto~~~

Taco Salad
Lettuce, Corn, Avocado~~~

...CHES

...ps.

Mayo.........$2.00

.................$3.00

...............$3.00

...ado, Mayo.......$3.00

...Aioli..................$3.00

.............................$3.00

...arette, Italian,

...outons........................$8.00

.................................$8.00

..., Red Onions..............$11.00

...cumbers,

...............................$12.00

...ans, Pico De Gallo...........$12.00

MILK SHAKES

Small	$2.00
Medium	$4.00
Large	$5.00

FLAVORS: Chocolate, Vanilla, Strawberry, Cherry, Peanut Butter and Jelly, Nutella, Cookies and Cream, Java Chip, Coffee, S'mores

Additional Toppings $1.00 EA: Chocolate Bits, Oreo Pieces, Cherries, Nuts, Peanut Butter, Nutella, Chocolate Syrup, Strawberry Sauce, Marshmallow, Whipped Cream

BETTY'S FAVORITE

HEALTH CENTER

During school hours, students feeling ill may obtain a pass to visit the health center, where a registered nurse is on duty. Students are not allowed to leave the building due to illness without the permission of a parent or guardian. Parents will be called and notified about the nature of any illness or injury. *Does this include a jingle jangle haze?*

Patient
Medical
Chart

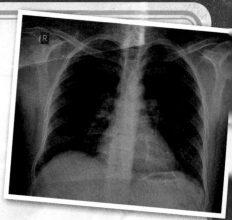

Patient Name: Fred Andrews
Sex: Male
Age: 45

Insurance Provided by: Andrews Construction

Description of Injuries:

- ☐ Bruises
- ☐ Concussion
- ☐ Broken bones
- ☐ Joints out of socket
- ☒ Loss of blood
- ☐ Burns
- ☐ Cuts or lacerations
- ☒ Gunshot wound

Cause of Injuries: Patient was attacked in Pop's Chock 'lit Shoppe by masked man.

LIBRARY

The library is open during the school day and during office hours. It offers a quiet place to conduct research, do homework, and work independently on personal projects.

Do I need a catchier title?

Riverdale: A Novel   by Jughead Jones

CHAPTER 1

Thicker than blood. More precious than oil. Riverdale's big business is maple syrup.

Since the town's founding, one family has controlled its lucrative syrup trade. The Blossoms. They were a part of the fabric of our daily lives. Rich or poor, old or young, we consumed Blossom syrup by the bucket. That sickly, sweet smell was inescapable.

Should I change the names to protect the not-so-innocent?

Need a better transition here. What am I leaving out?

The death of Jason Blossom precipitated a crisis. With the heir apparent gone, who would inherit the family business one day? Certainly not Cheryl. It was a question that brought the wolves to Riverdale. And now the Blossoms were circling the wagons against possible attack from within their own ranks.

Winter had come early to Riverdale, brutal and unforgiving. But it would be nothing compared to the storm that was gathering. A storm of chaos named . . . Cheryl Blossom.

Normally, I'd be siccing the Blossom family attorneys on you for libel, you Morrissey-loving emo troll. But I kind of like this image.

PARENT INVOLVEMENT

See that, Mom?

We welcome parent involvement, and encourage participation in the PTA. Chairing fundraisers, advising student organizations, and offering support at competitions and performances are all great ways to show support. But we believe in fostering student independence, and do not condone parental interference in coursework.

RIVERDALE HIGH SCHOOL

HRS

EST. 1941

RIVE
HIGH SCH

WHERE A

Fred Andrews
Contractor

Mary Andrews
Attorney

FP Jones
Unknown

Alice Cooper
Advisor, *The Blue & Gold*

ONCE A BULLD

DALE
L ALUMNI

EY NOW?

Sierra McCoy
Mayor of Riverdale

Hermione Lodge
Shareholder, Lodge
Industries

Clifford Blossom
Owner, Blossom
Maple Farms

Hal Cooper
Editor, *The Riverdale
Register*

Penelope Blossom
Homemaker

WAYS A BULLDOG!

EXTRACURRICULARS
HARD PASS

We expect all students to participate in at least one after-school activity or <u>athletic team</u>. Whether you want to tread the boards with the thespian society, snap photos for the yearbook, play an instrument in the marching band, or create something beautiful with the art club, we're sure you'll find the perfect way to channel your creativity and passion. Or if you prefer physical activity over artistic endeavor, try out for one of Riverdale's premier sports teams, and <u>go for the gold</u>! Read on as we highlight some of our most illustrious clubs and teams.

Can't we just liberate ourselves from the tired dichotomy of jock or artist?

STUDENT GOVERNMENT

RHS has a representative student council made of annually elected officers. They are the governing body for all student clubs. So if you want to help make a difference at your school, run for office and make your voice heard!

★TEAM★
VARCHIE

GO BULLDOGS!
BULLDOG FOOTBALL

Think you have what it takes to tackle your way to the top? Try out for the Riverdale Bulldogs varsity football team. But fair warning: Coach Clayton expects total dedication from his players. Practices are early, often, and extreme.

WATER POLO

Not every high school is lucky enough to have a water polo team, let alone a state championship winning team. But with our brand-new Clifford H. Blossom Natatorium to practice in, our team has every chance of taking the trophy again this year.

Otherwise known as the Aquaholics. Though given how their captain died, maybe we should think up a new nickname...

MY DEAR SWEET JAY-JAY X

CHEERLEADING

Riverdale's cheerleading squad is known as the River Vixens. They lead pep rallies, cheer at athletic events, and galvanize school spirit with a mix of gymnastics, dance, and all-around perkiness.

Practice uniform

Spotless T-shirt
Ponytails
Short shorts
Knee socks

Game day uniform

Long, shiny locks
Pom-poms (can't look ratty)
Short skirts
Tight vests

Slay

Give orders,
don't take them

Intelligence
is hot

Keep your friends
close and your
frenemies closer

Put usurpers in
their place, at
your feet

Queen bees
when to use honey
and when to sting

Cheryl's rules for staying on top of
the cheerleading pyramid

ADVENTURE SCOUTS

Are you a natural leader? Do you have the urge to explore and the skills to survive in the wilderness? Then the Adventure Scouts may be the right club for you! Scouts learn orienteering, bird watching, plant identification, knot tying, observation skills, and so much more.

FEELING SCARED?
WANT PROTECTION?
CALL THE RED CIRCLE
TEXT OR CALL
555-0145

AUDIO VISUAL CLUB

The Audio Visual Club is made up of students who are interested in videography and audio recording. Members film theatrical productions, tape orchestral concerts, and video athletic events for posterity. Members should have a keen eye for interesting subject matter, and an unobtrusive manner, so as not to detract from the events they film.

Someone left a very interesting video on a flash drive deep in the woods. I wonder if anyone from the AV club filmed it?

JOSIE AND THE PUSSYCATS

Riverdale's preeminent super-group, Josie and the Pussycats, bring their signature style—and kitty cat ears—to every performance. These proud women write their own songs, rock the mic, and shred guitar. Formed when Josie McCoy, Valerie Brown, and Melody Valentine all worked together at Power Records, the group recently expanded to include newcomer Veronica Lodge.

"Fear Nothing"
Performed by Josie and the Pussycats
Written by Valerie Brown

We get lost, and we get found
Now we are here, we won't back down
Write this in the sky, we own the night
And we fear nothing.

Call us outrageous, playing in lasers
Lost in the moment, dancing in cages
Break out the big guns, hands on the trigger
Out on the front lines, courage is liquid.

When the sun goes down, we light up this town
Let your voice be loud
Shake down the airways, put this on replay
All you people get loud.

We get lost, and we get found
Now we are here, we won't back down
Write this in the sky, we own the night
And we fear nothing.

We get lost, and we get found
Now we are here, we won't back down
Write this in the sky, we own the night
And we fear nothing.

Sweet like a chaser, lips make us famous
Stares like we're naked, no one can tame us
Roll like a goddess, nothing can stop us
Pull down the stars, like we own tomorrow.

When the sun goes down, we light up this town
Let your voice be loud
Shake down the airways, put this on replay
All you people get loud.

We get lost, and we get found
Now we are here, we won't back down
Write this in the sky, we own the night
And we fear nothing.

We get lost, and we get found
Now we are here, we won't back down
Write this in the sky, we own the night
And we fear nothing.

Oh, oh-oh-oh-oh-oh
Oh-oh-oh-oh-oh
Oh-woah
Oh, oh-oh-oh-oh-oh
Oh-oh-oh-oh-oh.

We get lost, and we get found
Now we are here, we won't back down
Write this in the sky, we own the night
And we fear nothing.

'Cause we get lost, and we get found
Now we are here, we won't back down
Write this in the sky, we own the night
And we fear nothing.

Possible album names:
Pussycat Power
9 Lives
The Cat's Meow
Cat and Mouse
Purrfect Harmony

FEMALE STUDENT ASSOCIATION

We, the undersigned, have formed the Female Student Association to protect the interests and reputations of female students at Riverdale High. We believe girls have the right to pursue their educations without fear of vile rumors being spread about them. We refuse to put up with sexism or to be shamed for normal, healthy teenaged behavior. We just want to be treated equally and with respect.

Signed:

So if any privileged, despicable miscreants come for us, we will go scorched earth on them.

Cheryl Blossom

Betty Cooper

Melody Valentine

Veronica Lodge

Ethel Muggs

Josie McCoy

Tina Patel

Val Brown

Ginger Lopez

RIVERDALE HONOR ASSOCIATION

The Riverdale Honor Association serves to recognize students who demonstrate excellence in academics, service, leadership, and moral fiber. To qualify, students must maintain at least a 3.7 GPA, perform twenty hours of community service, and be recommended by at least one of your teachers.

Bet that doesn't include the time I caught B and V doing a little B and E to hunt down Chuck Clayton's dirty little secrets. Color me impressed!

DARK BETTY
LiVES!!

COMMUNITY SERVICE

Community Service Club is a unique opportunity for Riverdale High School to give back to the town. Students are welcome to join to help make a difference in people's lives. Projects may include helping at the Riverdale Food Bank, organizing activities with senior citizens, and working on Homes for the Homeless building sites.

LIES

We have volunteering opportunities with the Sisters of Quiet Mercy, a group home where disenfranchised teens will learn such virtues as discipline and respect and enjoy lives of quiet reflection and servitude. Interested students can sign up to be a Peer Assistance Leader. PALs will be matched with a troubled teen, exchange letters, visit them in the Garden of Deliverance, and participate in monthly outings, which may include trips to the bowling lanes, putt-putt golf course, or Bijou theater for a movie.

For this school year, our main focus will be joining the Sweetwater River Cleanup Commission to help clean and protect the Sweetwater River.

Activities will include:

- ► Fund-raising to pay for environmental testing of the water
- ► Helping to organize volunteers for the town's Cleanup Day
- ► Creating an educational pamphlet about why keeping the river clean matters
- ► Leading town-hall style meetings to address our neighbors' concerns

CAMPUS LIFE

We have an extensive network of services and policies designed to help students make the most of campus life. RHS is committed to providing programming to promote learning and growth beyond the classroom.

RIVERDALE
SHERIFF'S DEPARTMENT

CITATION
Ticket No. 00000005789358

County: Rockland

City: Riverdale

Name: Cheryl Blossom

Address: Thornhill

Location of Offense: Riverdale High School

Type of Offense:
- ☐ Parking
- ☐ Speeding
- ☐ Littering
- ☐ Vandalism
- ☐ Truancy
- ☐ Public indecency
- ☑ Other

If other, please explain: Obstructing justice and inhibiting a criminal investigation

Listen up, fives, a ten is speaking! There is no campus life at Riverdale without Cheryl Blossom. Did you really think you could have a party without inviting moi?

CELL PHONES AND SOCIAL MEDIA

While cell phones are permitted on campus, students are prohibited from using them during class. They must be turned off and stored away during school hours, and may not be used in conjunction with coursework.

We understand that participation in social media is important to our students, but we ask that you relegate it to after school, and maintain decency and decorum when posting about yourselves or your fellow students.

GOING OFF-CAMPUS

Students are not permitted to go off-campus during school hours. We know you enjoy going to Pop's Chock'lit Shoppe for lunch or sneaking away to Lover's Lane, but that is expressly against school rules. Violators will be deemed truant and subject to suspension.

How I Spent My Summer Vacation
by Polly Cooper

I had big plans this summer. I was going to spend it with someone very close to me. We had decided to take a trip to a beautiful farm upstate with horses and a vegetable garden and acres and acres of wild land to explore. I was hoping to spend the season taking care of myself, as I've recently had some news about my health. And since my appetite has been up and down, we thought the farm would be the perfect place to lay low and let nature take its course. But I never took the trip. My "friend" never showed. And my parents decided I'd be better off spending the time with the Sisters of Quiet Mercy. And I couldn't stop them from sending me away. . . .

CARS AND PARKING

You must purchase a parking pass each semester to park in the Riverdale lot. Cars are not allowed to remain in the lot overnight. Students are not permitted to loiter in the lot during class hours. Stunts, racing, and vandalism to cars will not be tolerated.

Look what daddy bought Archikins!!!

VARIETY SHOW

The Riverdale Variety Show is a chance for our students to show off their many talents. This year the show will be hosted by ~~████████~~ *Kevin Keller* and will feature the following acts:

Josie and the Pussycats - Headlining Musical Act

Dilton Doiley - Knot Tying

Moose Mason - Stand-up Comedy

Ethel Muggs - Baton Twirling

Principal Weatherbee - Magic Act

Archie Andrews - Original Song

"I'll Try"

Written and performed by Archie Andrews

Can you hear me?
Am I drowned out in the crowd? Are
you listening?
Or is everyone else too loud for you
to hear anything
Are you just gonna walk away?
Cause there are so many things I can
do but instead I'll say.

I'll try
I'll try
To let it go, let it roll right off my
back.
Yes, oh I'll try
I'll try
To let it go, let it go and never look
back this way.

Do you wanna be the one who points
and blames?
Makes us feel many things
'Cause in a word I can't explain
Why it hurts so much, you see
We weren't born with all this pain
I guess that's anything
That keeps living day by day.

And I'll try
I'll try
To let it go, let it roll right off my
shoulders.
Yes, I'll try
I'll try
To let it go, let it go and never
look back this way.

Back this way.

I'll try
I'll try
To let it go, let it roll right off my
shoulder
Yes I'll try
I'll try
To let it go, let it go and never
look back this way.
Never look back this way.

DANCES

Riverdale High hosts a number of school-sponsored dances throughout the year to ensure our students can let off some steam and celebrate all of their hard work. The Semi-Formal is a back-to-school gala to kick off the start of a new year. And homecoming is the perfect time to cheer on our Riverdale Bulldogs, elect a homecoming king and queen, welcome back Riverdale alumni, and dance the night away!

c'est moi obvs.

Playlist

Him & I by G-Eazy & Halsey
Greatest Love Story by LANCO
What About Us by Pink
Tell Me You Love Me by Demi Lovato

No Promises by Cheat Codes
It Ain't Me by Kygo
Too Good at Goodbyes by Sam Smith

THE BLUE & GOLD

SUSPECT ARRESTED
FOR RIVERDALE MURDER

by Betty Cooper

Riverdale homecoming was spoiled by the news that Forsythe Pendleton "FP" Jones II has been arrested for the murder of student Jason Blossom. Sources tell this reporter that evidence may have been planted. On a night when alumni return to celebrate their alma mater, Northside prejudice against a former student from the Southside may have put an innocent man in jail.

'Read my glossed lips. Totally gonna happen.

BATTLE OF THE BANDS

Rockland County's annual Battle of the Bands is a highlight of the school year. Last year, our own super-group Josie and the Pussycats took the first-place trophy. Can they repeat that feat this year? We hope the whole student body will come out to support them!

COLLEGE NIGHT

We host an annual college night for our students to meet recruiters from top universities. Whether you're interested in pursuing your education at an Ivy League school or staying closer to home at prestigious institutions like Carson College, we aim to help you fulfill all of your collegiate aspirations.

Looks like someone is making other plans for their future.

PARTIES

While we cannot prevent them, off-campus parties without adult supervision are strictly prohibited. Anyone caught participating in an event that includes illegal activities will be placed on immediate suspension. Our advice: Better safe than sorry!

Cheryl's Party Fouls

DON'T spin the bottle unless you're ready to pucker up.

DON'T have a Britneyesque meltdown if a boy just isn't that into you.

DON'T do anything to ruin your makeup.

DON'T let party crashers rain on your parade.

DON'T drive yourself home. Find a buddy.

DON'T be the last to leave. No one likes a lurker.

Veronica's Favorite Party Games

Seven Minutes in Heaven
Truth or Dare
Never Have I Ever
Spin the Bottle
Secrets and Sins

Actually, I'm never playing that
one again. Some secrets should
remain hidden forever.

Party crashers? Please. I keep
it inner circle only.

RIVERDALE
FROM THE OFFICE OF THE MAYOR

Students of Riverdale,

May I be the first to wish you a productive and successful school year. I believe the children are our future. It is vital to the health of our fair city that you learn everything you can now. Because before too long, you will be the leaders of our community, making decisions that impact the town and one another. And you'll need a strong educational foundation based on honesty, fairness, and care for your neighbor's well-being to make the right choices. The whole town of Riverdale is counting on you!

Sincerely,

Sierra McCoy

Mayor of Riverdale
September 2018

THE BLUE & GOLD

THE WEEKLY NEWSPAPER OF RIVERDALE HIGH SCHOOL

SODALE DEVELOPMENT APPROVED BY MAYOR McCOY

by Betty Cooper

he Twilight Drive-In is closing its doors. Mayor Sierra McCoy approved the sale
f the property last week to an anonymous buyer. SoDale, the controversial new
evelopment planned for the site on Riverdale's Southside, promises to revitalize a
truggling neighborhood. But sources say that the buyer may have lined the mayor's
ockets to get the deal pushed through. Mayor McCoy declined to comment, but
s reporter will be watching her re-election campaign donation records closely.

SUPERLATIVES

Navigating the social scene is a complicated part of any student's high school experience. To make it easier for you, we've included some tried and true superlatives to help you keep track of your new classmates.

VERONICA LODGE
~~BEST DANCER~~

Biggest Daddy issues

ARCHIE ANDREWS

~~MOST LIKELY TO LEND A HELPING HAND~~

Most Likely to Make Out with a Teacher

87

SUPERLATIVES

KEVIN KELLER *Most Likely to Date a Bad Boy*
~~BIGGEST GOSSIP~~

BETTY COOPER
~~MOST LIKELY TO SUCCEED~~

Most Likely to Embrace the Dark Side

MOOSE MASON
~~HARDEST WORKER~~ *Most Surprising Cheater*

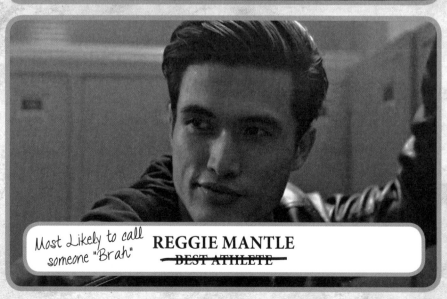

Most Likely to call someone "Brah" **REGGIE MANTLE**
~~BEST ATHLETE~~

SUPERLATIVES

Most Likely to Ditch Her

JOSIE McCOY
~~BEST PERFORMER~~

Backup for a Solo Career

JUGHEAD JONES
~~MOST INDEPENDENT~~

Most Likely to Join a Biker Gang

Most Likely to Nerd His Way Into a
Washington, DC, Internship

DILTON DOILEY
~~BEST SURVIVAL SKILLS~~

ETHEL MUGGS
~~SHYEST SMILE~~

Most Likely to Throw Down with a Milk shake

SUPERLATIVES

CHERYL BLOSSOM
~~QUEEN BEE~~

Most likely to steal your heart ## TONI TOPAZ
~~EDGIEST STYLE~~

92

VALERIE BROWN Most Likely to
~~MOST MUSICAL~~ Hold a Grudge

Most Likely **MELODY VALENTINE**
to Stay Quiet ~~PRETTIEST EYES~~

93

SUPERLATIVES

CHUCK CLAYTON

~~FOOTBALL STAR~~

Most Likely to Be Handcuffed in a Hot Tub

JASON BLOSSOM

~~MOST WELL-ROUNDED~~

RIP

IN MEMORIAM

We would like to remember one of our talented students who was taken from us too soon. Jason Blossom was an exemplary student, a gifted athlete, and a leader at Riverdale High School. He will be sorely missed. We include a memory that his twin sister, Cheryl Blossom, has agreed to share with the Riverdale community in honor of her brother:

"Even though we were twins, I used to demand I have my own birthday party. Until one year, out of the blue, Jason convinced me we had to combine them into one. It wasn't until years later, I found out why. It was because no one wanted to come to mine. And Jason didn't want me to know. He protected me. Every single day. I wish, that day at the river, I had protected him. I'm so sorry, Jay-Jay. We failed you. All of us."

— CHERYL BLOSSOM

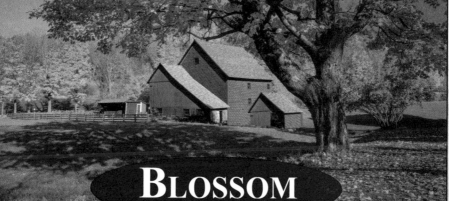

Come Clean Your River!

Join your neighbors in keeping the Sweetwater River looking and smelling sweet.
Volunteer on Saturday, September 16.
10:00 a.m. to 4:00 p.m.

ROVING EYE
NIGHTCLUB

DJ Sweet Tuesdays
$15 cover
Doors Open at 10:00 p.m.

The Pembrooke

Quality. Always.
Luxury living in Riverdale.
Showings by appointment only.

GUITAR FOR SALE

'84 Les Paul electric guitar in cherry red

$250 or best offer

Email archie@riverdale.com

Sunnyside
Trailer ~~Park~~ TRASH

You may not find a house in every place you roam,
But when you park at Sunnyside, you'll always be at home.

Affordable plots on Riverdale's Southside.

NOTES

A typical weekend in Riverdale means:

On Friday nights, football games then tailgate parties at the Mall-Mart parking lot

Saturday night is movie night, regardless of what's playing at the Bijou. And you better get there early, because there isn't any reserved seating in Riverdale.

And Sunday nights? Thank God for HBO.

NOTES

"Ode to the Twilight Drive-In"
by Jughead Jones

Your screen showed classics, new and old.
Your popcorn glistened with salt.
The perfect place to catch a flick
Or drink a chocolate malt.

The crowds, they came for years and years,
But now the sun is setting
And no one comes to see the shows.
And that won't change, I'm betting.

So now it's time to close your doors
Despite how hard I tried.
I am now without a home,
A Riverdale legend has died.

If someone comes to your house
and disrespects you, do what I do:
Burn it to the ground.

NOTES

"These Are the Moments I Remember"

written by Archie Andrews
performed by Josie and the Pussycats
with Archie Andrews at the 75th
Anniversary Jubilee

Every moment we're together
Is a moment I remember.
I'll take the good, the bad, the better.
And the smell of your favorite sweater.
These are moments I remember.
These are moments I remember.

My love, my heart,
I wanna share it with you.
Tough breaks, new starts,
I wanna share it with you.
I wanna share it with you.

When there's nothing left that's certain,
Then it's time to raise the curtains.
Whispers of a truth that shatters,

Dove deep to collect the errors.
These are moments we'll remember.
These are moments we'll remember.

My love, my heart,
I wanna share it with you.
Tough breaks, new starts,
I wanna share it with you.
When it seams too hard to bear,
I'll be here or I'll be there.
I wanna share it with you.

What's come undone
Can be built up,
Stronger than ever before.

My love, my heart,
I wanna share it with you.
Tough breaks, new starts,
I wanna share it with you.
When it seems too hard to bear,
I'll be here or I'll be there.
I wanna share it with you.
I wanna share it with you.

NOTES

Southside Serpents vs. Ghoulies: Know the difference.

Serpents

Hang out at the Whyte Wyrm
and Sunnyside Trailer Park

Leather jackets and frayed denim

Ride motorcycles

Use intimidation and muscle

Ghoulies

Loiter on street corners and in dark alleys

Studs and skulls

Drive hot rods

Traffic jingle-jangle